Jack
with the
Curly Tail

HOME IS WHERE THE HEART IS

Michelle E. Brown

Ellie
Home
will always
be forever
in your
heart

Michelle B

AuthorHouse™
1663 Liberty Drive
Bloomington, IN 47403
www.authorhouse.com
Phone: 833-262-8899

Because of the dynamic nature of the Internet, any web addresses or links contained in this book may have changed since publication and may no longer be valid. The views expressed in this work are solely those of the author and do not necessarily reflect the views of the publisher, and the publisher hereby disclaims any responsibility for them.

This book is printed on acid-free paper.

ISBN: 978-1-6655-2404-9 (sc)
ISBN: 978-1-6655-2405-6 (e)
ISBN: 978-1-6655-2406-3 (hc)

Library of Congress Control Number: 2021908349

Print information available on the last page.

Published by AuthorHouse 05/11/2021

authorHOUSE®

Dedicated to my family

Safiya
Terrance and Kizzy
Eric and Stephanie
Tanagra and Harold
And Ojetta
And Jack with the Curly Tail of the Brackney/Howell pack

Even with my ears covered I could still hear the big boom that came with all of the colored lights in the sky.

Skipper poked her nose under the chair and gave me a nudge. "Don't be afraid Jack," she said. "It's just fireworks to celebrate the country's birthday."

"Country was born today too?" I asked. When my brother, sisters and I were born there was a big boom and pretty colors in the sky. Even though I did not know where they were, I still remembered playing with them at the house on Charlotte Street. That seemed like such a long time ago.

"Is Country a puppy? Is Country a boy or girl? Can I meet her or him?" I asked.

"I don't know what Country is, Jack, but every year Mama Shari and Mama Lena have a birthday party" she said. "This is a special, fun day and now it can be your birthday party too!"

It was a special day full of surprises!

Skipper had woke me up with a big wet kiss.

"Wake up Jack! Time to get up. We're having a party today and there's a lot to do." She gave me another kiss and a little nudge to make sure I did not go back to sleep.

Mama Lena and Mama Shari were in the yard hanging colorful ornaments on the fence and tree. They had put a long table outside and covered it with a red, white and blue tablecloth.

Every now and then Mama Shari would go to the big black thing and open it to look at the food. It smelled so good. I wanted to take a peek but Mama Shari stopped me.

"No Jack! You can't get up here. The grill is for cooking and very hot." She said.

I was not sure what all that meant but just then I saw a flame flare up around the meat. I knew what that was. It was fire and I ran as far away from the black fire pot as fast as I could.

I was still shaking from fear when Skipper came out of the house. "What's the matter, Jack" she asked.

I could barely get the words out. "Fire! Over there! Fire!" I cried.

"Calm down Jack. It's alright. Humans use fire to cook with," she said. "Mama Shari and Mama Lena are very careful with that fire pot. They can tame the fire.

"See!" she said as Mama Shari sprinkled water on the flame making it go back down deep inside the fire pot. She turned the meat over then put the top back on the pot.

"The fire pot gets very hot" Skipper said "and can burn your paws. So, it's best to stay far away from it."

"Don't worry Skipper. I will." I said.

"Well let's go inside and get ready for the party" Skipper said turning around to go in the house. I followed her into the little room she called our closet.

Ever since the new pet store opened Skipper had started filling our closet with what she called "Accessories."

She pulled down a red hat with USA on the front for herself and a red, white and blue bandana for me.

"Perfect!" she said smiling, looking at her selections. She picked them up and took them to Mama Lena.

Mama Lena liked this "accessory" stuff. Every time we went to the pet store she and Skipper would find something new.

Mama Lena put the hat on Skipper gently pulling her ears through the two little holes and fastening the strap to her collar. "Come on Jack, you're next" she called.

There was no use resisting so I walked over and let her tie the bandana around my neck.

"Just look at you two. So cute!" she said. "I have to have a picture."

Pictures came with accessories. Every time Mama Lena put on our accessories, she would get the little box that flashed light and made me see little dots.

After the picture Skipper and I went back in the yard.

Our friend Busta Cat was watching from the tree in the yard.

Skipper looked up and said "Well what do you think? Perfectly accessorized for the party. You really should try it Busta."

"I wear my fur suit. That's it. A shiny black fur suit perfect summer, winter, spring and fall. Just right for all occasions. I'm a cat. Accessories, Yuk!" He scoffed.

"Oh Busta, you must try it. Accessories make me feel so pretty, happy and gay. They make every day special." She said. "Look at Jack. That bandana is just the right touch."

I did not say anything because Skipper would have her way no matter what. I just looked at Busta Cat and smiled. .

Just then the doorbell rang and our guests began to arrive for the party.

Alyssa and Big Boy were first through the gate. I tried to hide so Big Boy wouldn't see me accessorized but Alyssa saw me first. "Look at Jack in his bandana, Big Boy. Isn't he cute? I should get you one." She giggled.

Skipper smiled, looking at Big Boy. "I may have an extra one in the closet. What color would you like Big Boy?" she asked with a smile.

"Thanks, but no thanks Skipper." Big Boy replied shaking his head from side to side.

Busta Cat was still in the tree watching. He called out "That's right brother. Stick to the fur suit. Works for me."

Skipper turned and snarled "That's quite enough Mr. Busta Cat. Don't hate on those who have a flair for fashion."

More guests began to arrive.

There was Casandra and Mercedes with their little dogs Zachary and Corey.

Rocco came in with his long green iguana, Iggie and his puppy Balboa.

Jessie and Jackie, the twins, brought their twin parrots, Molly and Polly. Molly and Polly could say hello in human talk.

And Busta Cat's buddies Charli, Dinko and Spider came to the party with their humans Rashid, Hector and Maria.

All of the parents came with bowls of food. Each family wore special clothes that were as brightly colored as the fireworks that would light up the sky.

But instead of a big boom these bright colors came with laughter, music and wonderful smells.

Hector's father hung a giant toy from a branch of the tree.

"What's he doing Skipper?" I asked. "That's for the children. It's called a piñata and filled with candy." She explained.

"I hope he brought one for us" she said and walked over to sniff the bag laying on the ground.

Mr. Rodriguez reached in the bag and brought out another decorated like a big ball with long ribbons that reached the ground and hung it from a lower branch. It smelled like doggie treats and other good stuff.

"I didn't forget you and the others, Skipper," he said. Skipper laid down at his feet, rolled over and let him rub her belly.

Big Boy had come over to watch Mr. Rodriguez hanging the piñatas. "Yumbo!" he said licking his lips. "I hope it has the same treats as last time. That was fun and so delicious."

"What's in it" I asked.

"Oh, all kinds of treats for everybody – doggie treats, kitty snacks even something for Molly and Polly" Big Boy said.

Skipper trotted back over to where we were sitting. "This is going to be a wonderful party" she smiled.

And it was. Pretty soon the covers were taken off the food and everyone begin to eat.

Each person walked over to the fire pot and Mama Shari would open the lid. She asked each person "Burger, hotdog, chicken? We've got veggies and tofu on the other grill! Lena's handling that." Then she would reach into the fire pot with her long tool and put a piece of meat on each plate. Some people went right over to Mama Lena's fire pot to get their food.

Sometimes some food would fall to the ground and we took turns grabbing the treat.

Music played and as people finished eating, everyone – people and animals - began to dance. The children were given sticks and began hitting the star piñata until it broke and candy spilled out on the lawn.

"Your turn now" Mama Lena called and dangled our piñata ball.

All the pets, except for Iggie, came over to the ball. Molly and Polly sat on Jessie and Jackie's shoulders and watched as the dogs and some of the cats went after the ball.

The wind blew the ribbons on the ball all around but Zachary, Corey and Balboa each grabbed one and pulled with their teeth. They gave the ribbons a big tug and the ball burst open spilling all kinds of wonderful goodies on the ground for us.

Molly and Polly flew down and ate the seeds. Busta Cat even came down from the tree to grab a treat then climbed back up to his perch to watch the fun.

I found a chewy, my favorite and took it under the chair to watch.

Parties were fun.

Skipper found me under my chair. "Isn't the party grand" Skipper asked "and the best is yet to come."

I could not imagine anything else being more fun. My tummy was full. I had a chewy and was ready for a nap.

That's when the big boom and the lights in the sky started.

"Look, Look Jack. Isn't it wonderful" Skipper asked looking up at the bright lights in the sky.

"No. No." I whined and put my paws over my ears.

Finally, the lights and noise stopped. The guests began to leave. Skipper, Lena, Shari and I waved good-bye to everyone and went into our house.

Mama Lena and Mama Shari talked about all the fun everyone had had at the party. Skipper was still wide awake and sat on the couch between them listening.

Me, I was all tired out and ready to go to sleep. Mama Lena saw me sliding to the floor.

"I think someone is ready for bed! Looks like Jack has had enough excitement for one day." Mama Shari and Skipper looked my way. Mama Shari laughed but Skipper looked sad to have the day come to an end.

Mama Shari said, "Come on pups Time for bed!" She stood up and started walking towards the bedroom. I was right behind her then came Mama Lena.

Skipper stayed on the couch just in case they changed their mind and wanted to talk about the party more but finally she jumped down and followed everyone to the bedroom. Mama Lena took off our accessories and Skipper and I curled up in our bed.

"Well, what do you think Jack? How was your first fourth of July?' Skipper asked.

"Well I had lots of fun with all our friends. I liked the piñata. I ate so much and got a chewy." I said. "The fireworks were kind of scary but all and all it was a good day."

I curled up in the bed beside Skipper. My eye lids were growing heavy. "Good night Skipper. Good night Country. "I said with a great big yawn.

"Good night Jack and Happy Birthday." She said and gave me a big Skipper kiss. I snuggled up closer to her and went sound asleep.

The next morning Skipper came to get me up but I was already awake. I had got in my own bed and I was gnawing on my chewy from the piñata.

"Are you going to stay in bed all day?" she asked.

"I don't know Skipper. I hadn't thought about it. I was just having fun with my chewy. Do you want a bite?" I asked.

"It has slobber all over it Jack. That's so gross." She said. "Besides we're going to the pet store today and after that to the new dog park."

I wasn't too excited about the pet store. I didn't want to accessorize and take pictures today. I was still tired from the 4th of July birthday party but the dog park was something new.

"What's the dog park Skipper?" I asked perking my one ear up.

"It's a place to play and make new friends." She said. "I think I'll wear a bandana. What about you Jack?"

"Do I have to accessorize today Skipper? Can't I be just me – Jack?" I asked.

Skipper didn't say anything. She just turned, went to the closet and got two matching bandanas. She started walking towards Mama Lena saying, "We'll wear matching accessories that way everyone will know we're a family."

I picked up my chewy and followed Skipper into the other room. Maybe Mama Lena would take a picture of me with my chewy before it was all gone.

Mama Lena put on our bandanas then got out our travel bag. I ran over and put my chewy in the bag.

"Oh Jack, that's so cute. Stay right there while I take a picture" Mama Lena said. This time she used her talking box instead of the picture box.

Mama Shari had just come in the room with our leashes which meant we were going somewhere in the car.

"Look Shari! Jack wants to take his chewy. Isn't that cute?" She said and held up her talking box. I looked too. There I was with my chewy!

"How many pictures do you have of those pups Lena?" Mama Shari laughed.

"They're our babies Shari and they're so cute." Mama Lena laughed too.

Mama Shari took my chewy out of the bag. I started to cry.

"Don't cry Jack. You might lose your chewy at the park. So why don't you pick another toy to take, like your ball or the Frisbee." She said.

I really liked my ball and didn't want to lose my chewy. I could still chew on it for a couple of days. So, I ran over to the toy basket and got my yellow ball.

Skipper got the tugging toy out of the basket and we put them both into the travel bag.

"We're going to have so much fun at the dog park" Skipper said.

Her tail was wagging real fast. I wasn't so sure about the dog park but I liked riding in the car so my tail was wagging too.

Mama Lena put our leashes on and we hopped in the car. She made sure we were safe in the backseat.

"Everyone buckled up?" Mama Shari asked.

Mama Lena smiled and said "Yes."

Skipper and I barked.

"Well alrighty then. Let's get this adventure started" Mama Shari said starting the car and we were off to the dog park.

We drove right to the dog park. Skipper started to whine when we passed the pet store but Mama Shari promised, if we were good at the park, we would stop on our way home and each get a new toy.

Mama Lena laughed and said, "Maybe some new bandanas too!" Skipper barked "Yes, More bandanas!!"

"But Skipper, don't we have enough accessories already." I asked.

"We're going to make new friends at the dog park Jack. We will definitely need more accessories!" She smiled then poked her nose out the window so she could breathe in the fresh air.

I put my nose out the other window. The wind blowing on my face was the best part of car rides.

Pretty soon Mama Shari turned the corner and brought the car to a stop under a shady tree.

"Well here we are. Who's ready to have some fun and make new friends?" Mama Shari asked.

Skipper and I jumped up and down barking "We are! We are!"

"Look Jack! It's the dog park." Skipper barked. "We're going to have so much fun." Skipper couldn't wait to get out of the car to go in the dog park.

"Shari!!! Don't get them all worked up," Mama Lena fussed. "Settle down pups. Let me get your leashes and toys together then we can go in."

We both tried to sit down but it was hard to do because our tails were wagging too much.

Finally, Mama Lena had our things together and Mama Shari opened the door. We were at the dog park!!

The dog park was a lot like our backyard at home only way bigger.

There were lots of dogs with their parents. Some of the dogs were playing with their parents, catching Frisbees or pulling on tug toys. Other dogs were playing chase with each other. Everyone looked like they were having so much fun.

Our friends Corey and Balboa were there talking to some other dogs we didn't know. When Corey saw us. He ran to the gate to say hello. Balboa was right behind him

"Welcome to the dog park" they barked all at once. "Come and meet the gang" Balboa said.

Corey and Skipper took off running into the park but I stayed back by my Mamas.

Balboa asked, "What's wrong little dude?"

I told him about the dogs I had met before I found my family. I told them how they had been mean to me and called me names until Big Boy came along.

"Bullies, that's what they were Jack," Balboa said. "Big Boy got them told."

"I may not be as big as Big Boy but I'm a boxer." Balboa said. "See these white socks" He said lifting a paw. "See this chin" he said poking out his chin. My dad works at the gym with human boxers and I've picked up a thing or two. If somebody messes with you they'll have to deal with me."

Balboa licked my face. "I've got your back Jack. Come on in the park!"

Skipper came back to see if I was okay.

"Jack was just telling me about those bullies he met back in the day," Balboa said. "I told him not to worry. Big Boy comes to this park and when he's not here, I'll watch out for Jack."

"That's right. Don't worry Jack" Skipper said. "Everyone here is nice. You've got friends here already. And if anyone gets too frisky Mama Lena or Mama Shari will chase them off."

That made me feel better and I did want to play so I followed Skipper, and Balboa into the dog park.

"Jack! Hey Jack!" I heard someone calling my name. I looked around and saw Corey's brother, Zachary running across the dog park with his person Casandra.

Zachary's tail was wagging real fast. He was very excited. "First time at the park?" he asked. "You're going to love it here."

Casandra bent down and took Zachary off his leash. He looked over his shoulder and said "Come on Jack. Let me show you around."

I looked at Mama Lena and Mama Shari then at Skipper. Mama Shari and said "It's okay, Jack. Go play."

Skipper took off running after Zachary, Corey and Balboa. I had to run real fast to catch up.

First, we ran from tree to tree and played the "marking" game. Then Zachary took us over to meet a group of dogs.

No one said anything at first. They just sniffed the three of us and then we sniffed them. Zachary told us that was the way things were done at the dog park.

After the sniffing was done we all started to play – barking, jumping and running around the dog park.

When we got tired, Zachary, Skipper and I walked over to the fountain for a drink of water. I looked around for my Mamas.

I saw then standing by the fence talking to another dog mom. She was standing outside the park with a little dog who was getting ready to come in the park.

I looked at the little dog. He was about my size but he was different than me. He had accessories on his back legs but I had never seen accessories like his before.

I walked over to the fence and said hello. "Hi, I'm Jack. I like your accessories. Did you get them at the pet store?" I asked.

"Hi, my name is Doxey. What are accessories?" he asked.

"Oh, I'm sorry. I thought everyone calls them accessories," I said.

"That's what my sister Skipper calls all the extra things we wear over our fur suits. Mine is a bandana. What do you call yours?" I asked.

"Oh, now I understand" Doxey said laughing. "You mean my wheels. They're not accessories. They help me get around."

A tall skinny dog came over and gave Doxey the sniff.

"Hey Doxey! How you doing? You racing today?" he asked.

"Hi Grey! I have to see who is here, unless you're ready to take me on in a long-distance race." Doxie said with a laugh.

"I wish little dude but my racing days are over. Who's your new friend?" he said and came over to give me a sniff.

"I'm sorry!" Doxie said. "Jack, this is Grey. This is Jack's first time at the park. Grey is retired. He used to run races."

"Nice to meet you kid. Welcome to the park," He said then walked off.

Doxey took off running. I stood watching. His front legs moved like mine but the wheels moved for his back legs.

Doxey looked over his shoulder and said "Come on Jack! Let's play!"

We ran around and round the dog park at least three times. When we took a break, I asked Doxie if he liked to play with toys.

"I brought some with me. They're in the bag my moms have. That's them over there. Come on!" I said and started towards the fence.

Doxie stood back and watched them for a minute. "What's wrong" I asked.

"I have to watch humans. Sometimes they treat me funny." He said.

"My moms won't treat you funny. They are always nice to everyone." I told him.

Just then Doxie's mom came back and started talking to Mama Shari again.

She waved at Doxie and said "It's ok boy. Come over and meet my new friend."

Doxie smiled, then he and I walked over to the moms.

"It looks like our boys are friends too" she said and bent down and gave each of us a rub on the head.

Mama Lena bent over and rubbed our heads too.

"How long has Doxie been…." Mama Shari began to ask.

"Differently-abled?" Diane said. "Since he was just a baby."

I looked at the toy bag and barked. I was hoping Mama Lena would get out the pull toy so Doxie and I could play tug-of-war.

Mama Lena reached for the bag then turned and asked Diane. "Is it alright? I mean can he play like other dogs? I'm sorry I've just never seen…"

Diane finished for her. "A differently-abled dog. He can do just about anything any other dog can do. He just does it differently."

Mama Shari pulled out the tennis ball. "OK boys! How about a game of catch," she said throwing the ball.

Doxie and I took off running. He caught the ball the first time but the next time I got it.

After a while Diane and Doxie had to go home.

Mama Lena called Skipper. We all got in the car and headed home.

The dog park was fun. We had made many new friends.

I wanted to talk about it with Skipper but she was taking a nap. All that playing had made me tired too so I curled up on my side of the back seat to take a nap.

In no time at all, Mama Shari had the car back at our house and we were pulling into our yard.

Mama Lena had to wake Skipper up but I was already awake. I had been dreaming about my chewy and couldn't wait to get in the house.

I started to bark. "Come on Skipper. Wake up!" I barked.

"I am awake Jack" she snapped. "Would you mind getting off my head?"

I had noticed some people going into the house next to ours and had put my front paws on Skipper's head so I could see out the car window.

"Oh! I'm sorry Skipper but there's something going on out there. I was just trying to get a better look," I said and sat back down on the car seat.

About then Mama Lena opened the car door so we could get out of the car. She got our toy bag out of the car then went up on the porch and sat down beside Mama Shari.

I sat down beside them. I had wanted to get in the house so I could have my chewy but now I wanted to know what was going on next door.

Skipper went right over to the fence to get a better look.

Mama Shari called out to her "Skipper, come up here with us. Don't be so nosy!"

Mama Lena laughed, "That's our curious girl. She's going to see what's going on!"

Skipper walked back to the porch and sat down.

Busta Cat was in his favorite spot up in the tree.

"What's going on Busta Cat? I know you can see everything.", Skipper asked.

"Looks like you've got new neighbors," he said. "A man, woman, boy and a squirmy one, they have to carry. Can' tell if it's a boy or a girl but it looks like trouble!"

"What's trouble Busta Cat," I asked.

"Lots of noise. Getting chased around. Even pulling your tail when they're that little. They don't mean any harm, but I stay away until they are bigger. And the mothers always shooing you away, talking about germs and stuff. That's all. Just trouble." He said.

"Any new friends for us?" Skipper asked. "Think I saw some dog toys. And the man was checking the fence to keep them in and us out." Busta Cat said. "But no fence can stop me Skipper. I'll check it all out and let you know more later."

Mama Shari and Mama Lena seemed happy we had new neighbors so I was happy too!

After a while we went in our house. I got my chewy and hopped in my bed. Skipper came and sat down in her bed beside me.

"So, what did you think of the dog park Jack" she asked.

I told her it was fun and I was happy to see our old friends and make so many new friends at the dog park.

There was Doxey with his wheels. There was Grey with his stories about running faster than the wind before retiring. And Harry, who wore a sweater because he didn't have any hair on his body just his mohawk hair on the top of his head.

Skipper had made new friends too. Some even liked accessories as much as she did!!

"We didn't get to the pet store, but I had a great day." Skipper said. "And who knows, tomorrow we might make even more friends if Busta Cat is right about our new neighbors!

"But I thought Busta Cat said he saw Trouble," I said. "That can't be good."

"Silly Jack, not the trouble!" She laughed "He said there might be dogs. I hope they like accessories!"

Just then Mama Shari and Mama Lena came in to say good night. They pat each of us on the head and tickled our tummies.

"Good night pups! Sleep tight and don't let the bed bugs bite," Mama Shari said with a laugh.

I jumped out of my bed and barked. I grabbed it in my teeth and started shaking it as hard as I could. No bugs were going to bite me.

Mama Lena laughed. "Now see what you've started Shari!" She picked me up and gave me a big hug.

"It's ok Jack. There aren't any bugs. Mama Shari was just being funny!" She put me on the floor then fixed my bed and put a clean towel in it for me to lay on.

"It's all better now Jack." She said and patted the towel. "Come on time for bed little guy." I gave my mama a big kiss, jumped in bed and went sound to sleep.

Skipper was already up when I got up the next morning. She was standing up looking out the window.

"What do you see Skipper? And what's that noise," I asked.

"It's coming from next door, those new neighbors," she said.

"Is the Trouble making all that noise Skipper? Busta Cat said Trouble made noise," I asked.

"No, its not Trouble" Skipper said. "I see Hector's dad and some of his friends."

"Are we having another party Skipper? Does he have more treats?" I still had my chewy from the party but thought it would be nice to have another one for later.

"No Jack, it doesn't look like another party but he's talking to Mama Lena. Come on," she barked. "Let's go find out what's going on!"

Skipper took off running and I followed her right through our special doggie door out into the yard.

Mama Shari was standing by Hector's dad listening to him and Mama Lena talk.

"How high is this fence going to be, Jose and why do they feel the need for a privacy fence." She asked.

"I don't know the whole story Lena. I know they've had a rough time. Some wounds need time and space to heal. I guess they just need to feel secure, safe for their kids and their dogs." He said.

"Do we look dangerous Jose?" Mama Lena protested. "They don't even know what kind of people we are or how neighbors live on this block and they're building a fence!"

Mama Shari put her arm around Mama Lena's shoulder. "Let's give them time and a little space babe. We don't know their story. Remember when we first moved in we weren't sure how people would react to us - an inter-racial, gay couple – moving on to their block, but it worked out beautifully. This is home! Everybody's home!"

Mama Lena kicked at the wood for the fence. "I hear what you're saying but we took a chance. We believed in the goodness of people. We didn't build a fence!"

"Come on pups. Let's go in the house," she said and turned to go back to the house.

I wanted to stay outside and see what was going on but Mama Lena looked so sad I followed her and Skipper into the house.

Mama Lena sat in her big chair. Skipper climbed up on her lap. I went to our closet and pulled out two bandanas. Maybe if we put on our accessories and let Mama Lena take pictures that would make her smile.

Mama Shari came in the house. She got the car keys and our leashes.

"I think my family needs the dog park today! Come on Lena no moping about things we have no control over. It's going to be alright," she said and pulled Mama Lena up from the chair.

"But a fence Shari! It's got me feeling all kinds of emotions I don't like" Mama Lena said.

She saw the bandanas I had brought from the closet.

"Jack, you want to accessorize? Well, that's a first." she laughed and put our bandanas around our necks.

"I have to have a picture of this. Jack's first attempt at fashion,' She laughed.

Skipper barked "But they don't match!!" But Mama Lena took the picture anyway and we were off to the park.

The next morning, we woke up to a bang, bang thump coming from outdoors. Then there was a noise that made everything shake.

Skipper did not go to the window. She jumped out of bed and ran into the kitchen to find our mamas.

I ran into the living room and hid under Mama Lena's big chair.

All of the sudden the horrible noise stopped. I could hear Mama Shari talking to Hector's dad on the porch.

Then she came into the kitchen and started to talk to Mama Lena. I came out from under the chair and went in the kitchen and sat by Skipper.

I asked Skipper what was going on but she shushed me and said, "Just listen, Jack."

I heard Mama Lena ask "Now What? First a fence, now all this drama the first thing in the morning!" She was using her unhappy voice.

It wasn't the sad voice but the one she used when someone did something bad like when the kids called Hector a bad name, or when the man kept throwing the paper in the bushes instead of putting it on the porch.

She even used it one time for me when I thought her new shoes were a chew toy.

"It's an old house babe. Jose apologized for the noise but they're trying to get it together so the family can move in." Mama Shari was saying. "And you know how it is with his guys, they all volunteer for the housing rehab program so when he can get a crew together he takes full advantage of the work day. Don't hold it against the family. They're going to be our new neighbors."

"You're right Shari. So, what did you learn about our new neighbors?" Mama Lena asked.

Mama Shari came over to the table and sat down. She reached over and gave Mama Lena's hand a squeeze. Then she looked at Skipper and I and asked if we wanted to know about the new neighbors too.

Skipper barked and put her paws on Mama Shari's lap.

I scooted over closer to Mama Lena. I wanted her to talk with her happy voice so I kissed her hand.

"Well, it's a couple about our age Babe. They have a son and a daughter. The little girl is just a toddler." She said then looking a Skipper added "And yes they have two dogs Miss Skipper!"

Skipper barked "I need more details Mama. Something Busta Cat doesn't know yet!'

"They're in temporary housing now but the plan is to be moved in next door in time for the boy to start school this fall. Jose says they are good people who have seen some bad times. He thinks they'll fit in good once they get settled." Mama Shari got up and went to the cupboard and got a treat for Skipper and me.

I took my treat and went back by Mama Lena to eat.

Skipper sat down and looked at Mama Shari. She wouldn't take her treat at first.

She was mad because Mama Shari did not give her anything she could tell Busta Cat first.

"Well if you don't want it" Mama Shari said and started to put the treat back in the bag.

Skipper wasn't that mad. She barked and took the treat from Mama Shari's hand after doing the paw shake trick.

"And the fence?" Mama Lena asked. It wasn't in her happy voice but she wasn't unhappy either.

"It's a fence babe! They're not building a wall or asking us to pay for it," Mama Shari said with a laugh. "Once we get to know each other maybe it will come down or at least have a little gate."

Later on, Skipper and I went out in our yard to play.

Busta Cat was in his favorite spot in the tree. He was licking his paws.

When Skipper walked by the tree he called down and asked "Want to share anything Skipper? I know you know something. I saw Hector's dad on your porch."

"I'll tell, if you tell. What you have found out Busta Cat", she answered.

"I don't have much. Just been watching the humans work. Haven't seen the family. Maybe they changed their mind." He said and went back to licking his paws.

Skipper smiled and did her happy dance.

She barked "At last I beat you Busta Cat. I know something you don't." She barked some more and kept doing her dance.

"Well are you going to keep up all the noise or spill it" Busta Cat snarled. "I've got things to do" he said and started to climb down the tree.

Skipper stopped dancing. "Wait, I'm going to tell you. It just felt good to know something first."

She sat down and told Busta Cat what we had learned from Mama Shari.

"So, you see they haven't changed their mind. They'll be here so the boy can go to school and Trouble's name isn't trouble its Toddler and Toddler is a girl." She finished.

Busta Cat just shook his head and said, "Good work Skipper for a dog." Then he walked off.

Skipper growled and started to chase Busta Cat "Good work for a dog!! I'll show you good work for a dog."

Busta Cat laughed and hopped over the fence.

I laughed a little too!

Skipper was funny sometimes.

Every day the humans would come and work on the house.

There was a big, tall fence up between the yards that only Busta Cat could see over from his spot in the tree.

Skipper and I would sit very close and just listen.

We did not hear any dogs yet but some days we would hear Hector's dad singing.

Skipper and I would throw our heads back and sing along.

Skipper told me to do the marking game on the big, tall fence so the dogs would know we were there.

I told her I would wait until we could play the sniffing game with them too, like we did at the dog park.

When the human men made too much noise Mama Shari would get our things and we would go to the dog park.

One day we stopped at the pet store.

Skipper went right to the accessories. She picked out some new bandanas.

Mama Lena smiled. Accessories made her happy too.

I saw a ball and some chewies. That made me happy.

Mama Shari got our food and pushed the basket. I don't think the pet store made her too happy but she was happy just to be with us.

Some days there were lots of cars at the dog park and we had to wait to get our shady spot.

One day when we got to the park Skipper was looking out the window she said "Look Jack. There's some more new dogs!"

I was laying on the seat chewing on my new toy.

I looked out of my window at the park but I didn't see anybody new.

"Where Skipper? I see Big Boy, Corey, Missy, Zachary, Puffy, Balboa, Doxie, Grey and Harry but no one new."

"In that car Jack," she said. "The one that was in our shady spot. See them in the back!"

The car was moving away but I could see two heads.

"Will they come back Skipper? We didn't get to play the sniffing game." I asked.

"Maybe another day. Let's go in and see what the gang knows about them" she said and ran off to join the other dogs.

Doxie came over to play with me. He was my very best friend at the dog park.

He told me there had been lots of new dogs at the park that morning. He told me all about them.

I was so excited. Maybe today I knew something first, even before Skipper, to tell Busta Cat!

Doxie and I played and ran all around the park. He introduced me to some of his friends that were differently-abled too.

Rex had three legs but he could run almost as fast as Doxie. Rex told me to be careful around cars. "Sometimes the humans can't control the cars and they can hurt you if you get in their way."

Lexi could not see too good but she could sniff better than all the other dogs. "I can smell my dad coming home before he even gets there. Nothing gets past this nose," she said and sniffed the air. "I think I smell rain coming."

After a while the mamas called us. It was time to go home.

I couldn't wait to tell Skipper about my new friends and hear about her new friends too. Maybe she knew about the dogs in the car.

We had both played so much that instead of talking when we got in the car we both curled up to take a nap.

Mama Lena looked at us in the back seat and laughed "Playing is hard work. Isn't it pups? Go ahead and take your nap."

Mama Shari laughed too. "Next time around I'm coming back as a dog Lena – your dog. You've got those two-spoiled rotten. Breakfast snacks, shopping, playing, napping then dinner with all those kisses and belly rubs mixed in. I want a dog's life."

Both mamas were laughing. They were happy. Skipper was happy and I was happy. I closed my eyes and went to sleep.

When we got home Skipper and I went to sit by the big, tall fence to see if we could sing with Hector's dad but it was quiet on the other side.

Skipper walked over to the tree to see if Busta Cat was in his perch but he wasn't there.

We lay down in the shade under the tree and talked about the dog park.

I told her about my new friends Rex and Lexi.

She told me what the other dogs had been talking about. Her friend Puffy had been to the pet store too and had a new accessory collar.

"It was so sparkly and pretty Jack. I have to get one next time we go," she said.

The dogs that were in the car were named Serenity and Pax. They were new to the neighborhood and had only stayed in the park a short time. They had come with their dad and boy.

"Do they have a Mama? Do they like to play tug of war? Did they have a ball?" I had lots of questions but just then Busta Cat came back to his perch.

He had been on the other side of the big tall fence.

"Good afternoon Busta Cat. Jack and I were just sitting here talking about our fun at the dog park" Skipper said.

"Fun at the dog park, you say. Well I guess you aren't interested in my news." Busta Cat said. "I guess I'll just take a nap."

He started to curl up for a nap but Skipper began to bark.

"Don't you dare go to sleep Busta Cat! Spill it! What's going on over there?"

At first Busta Cat acted like he was sleep. Skipper kept barking until he opened his eyes to talk.

"So, you want to hear what Busta Cat knows, Miss Skipper. Not trying to be first today are you," he purred.

"Well, I saw them all today. The man, the woman, the boy, the toddler, the two dogs and most importantly their cat Miss Midnight," he began. "She's a house cat so we won't be patrolling the neighborhood but we talked at her window. She's quite the mouser."

"And the dogs?" Skipper asked.

"Oh yeah, them – the dogs. Well, there's two. One kind of looks like you Jack. They didn't try to chase me. Miss Midnight says they're friendly. Welcomed her right into the family," Busta Cat said.

"When can I see them, Busta Cat? Will the boy play with us?" I asked.

"I don't know all that Jack. My source, Miss Midnight, says they're not sleeping over there yet. Still working but real soon." Busta Cat purred. "Can I take my nap now?"

Hector's dad was sitting in the kitchen with Mama Lena and Mama Shari when Skipper and I went in the house.

"Well tomorrow's the big day ladies. I am doing the finishing touches today." He said. "They're good folks. They want to be good neighbors. Had me put in a dog run on the other side of the yard so their dogs wouldn't disturb you. Boy's a great kid, a little sad but I know he'll cheer up now that they have a real home. And the little one, she's cute as a button".

"I'm feeling better about the whole thing Jose. All that drama over the fence was just a knee jerk reaction." Mama Lena said.

"What drama over what fence," Hector's dad laughed.

He got up and hugged both Mamas.

"Come here pups! I got some love for you too." He said.

He took a dog biscuit out of his pocket for each of us, patted us on our heads then went out the door.

Skipper smiled and did her happy dance.

"What kind of biscuit did he give them Shari? Skipper doesn't get that happy over the biscuits we buy? Maybe we should switch" Mama Lena said.

The biscuits were pretty good but I knew why Skipper was dancing.

She had another first on Busta Cat. The neighbors weren't coming soon. They were coming tomorrow.

Skipper couldn't wait to go out and share her news with Busta Cat!

The next morning there was lots of human noise coming from the other side of the big tall fence.

We heard Hector's dad's voice and some of the voices from other days. We even heard Hector but there were new voices too.

Busta Cat had gone over the fence to visit with his friend Miss Midnight and to see what was going on.

We heard lots of talking and singing and laughing. Then we heard barking!

Skipper and I ran back and forth on our side of the big, tall fence.

"Hello! Hello! I'm Skipper!'

"Hi, I'm Jack! What's your names?" I asked. I tried to jump really high so I could see over the fence but it was too high!!

We barked and barked but the dogs didn't answer us. Maybe it was because we didn't do the sniffing game first.

Then I heard the lady say "Come on dogs. Let's go to the park while the men work."

"Can I stay here and help Dad? And play with Hector too?" we heard one of the voices say.

"That's the boy" I told Skipper.

"How do you know that's the boy Jack?" she asked.

"Because I used to have a boy before I was Jack and that's what boys sound like." I said.

We heard car doors shut and the dogs were gone.

"Do you think they're going to our dog park Skipper?" I asked. "Do you think our mamas will take us to our dog park today? Do you think they'll be our friends?"

I was barking and jumping. Skipper was barking too.

Mama Lena came to the door and called us in to the house. I was hoping she would say "Let's go to the dog park right now" but instead she sat in her big chair to read the paper.

I ran through the house looking for Mama Shari. She would take us to the park but I couldn't find her.

I got my chewy, climbed in our big dog bed and thought about our new friends.

I wondered if the boy would be our friend too, like my old boy was. I remembered how my old boy and I would play ball together. I hope this boy would let me play ball with him and his dogs.

Skipper came in our room and asked what I was doing.

"Just chewing and thinking Skipper. Want a bite of my chewy?" I asked.

"It's got slobber all over it Jack. That's so gross. Scoot over." She said.

Skipper climbed in our big dog bed with me. " Ok, tell me what you were thinking Jack and give me a piece of that chewy from the clean end."

I gave her a piece of the chewy from the clean end and told her about playing with my old boy when I was puppy and how I hoped that the dogs and the boy would be our new friends.

When we went to the dog park the next day our friends told us that the new dogs Serenity and Pax had been there the day before.

Big Boy was at the park. He said he had played the sniffing game with Serenity and Pax. "That Serenity's a cutie!"

When he saw Skipper's ear's go up, he added "But not as cute as you Skipper! Nobody's as cute as you Skipper!"

That made Skipper smile. Big Boy liked Skipper special. When he saw her smile, he told us more about the dogs. "They're both pretty fun. And that Pax is something else."

"Something else? I thought Pax was a dog too! What is Pax – a cat, a bird? Does Pax look like Iggie the iguana? Is Pax differently-abled like my friend Doxie?'" I asked Big Boy.

"Slow down Jack! Pax is a dog too. Serenity says Pax brought peace to their family's house after some bad times. Didn't want to call a dog Peace so they picked Pax. Means the same thing Serenity says." Big Boy told us.

"Does Serenity like accessories? Is Pax a boy or girl? Where do they live? Did you tell them about me?" Skipper asked.

"Don't know all of that Skipper but they live in the neighborhood. I figure they'll meet you soon enough so you can introduce yourself" Big Boy shrugged.

Puffy had been listening to Big Boy talk. She had on her sparkly collar.

"Well Serenity asked about my collar Skipper. So, I think she likes accessories" Puffy said.

We played at the park for a little while then went to the pet store. We got more accessories and some toys.

We could hear all kinds of noise at the big, tall fence when we got in our yard.

We could hear the dogs too.

Skipper and I ran from one end of the fence to the other saying hello!

"Hello! Hello! It's Skipper and Jack" Skipper barked.

"I'm Jack! Hello it's me" I barked.

This time the dogs barked back.

I let Skipper do the talking. She asked them their names. It was Serenity and Pax.

"You've been going to our dog park. Our friends told us about you" Skipper said.

"It's your park? Are you rich? Is it ok that we went there?" one of the dogs asked.

Skipper laughed. "It's not my park. It's our park. The park where all the dogs in our neighborhood go to play. Now it's your park too!"

"Pax and I have lived in some unfriendly places so it's best to ask." Serenity said.

Skipper and Serenity kept talking about the park, accessories and other things.

I went closer to the fence and said "Are you there Pax? I'm Jack. I have a curly tail. I can jump really high and I can do lots of things but not too good. That's why they call me Jack. I hope you will be my friend."

"I'm here Jack. I have a curly tail too. I would like to be your friend." Pax said.

Just then Mama Lena called us in the house. I said goodbye to Pax and Skipper said good bye to Serenity.

I didn't get to talk to Pax when Skipper and I went out in our yard later but we could hear the family playing.

The humans were laughing at the boy and Toddler. They were playing with the dogs. Pax and Serenity were barking. It sounded like so much fun.

I looked in the tree for Busta Cat. I wanted to ask him about Pax's curly tail. I wanted to ask him if Toddler pulled Pax's tail. I wanted to ask Busta Cat all kinds of questions but he wasn't on his perch in the tree.

Maybe tomorrow we could meet them at the dog park and get to play the sniffing game.

Skipper and I talked about our new friends when we got in our beds.

I told Skipper next time we went to the pet store I was going to get chewies to share with Serenity and Pax.

Skipper said she would like to get a bandana for Serenity but didn't know what color to get. "That big tall fence is in the way. How will we be able to share with them Jack?" she said.

Our mamas turned the light off because it was time to sleep.

I had a big scary dream. I always had dreams but most of time the dreams were about playing with Skipper, my chewy or running.

I didn't know it was a big scary dream until Skipper woke me up. Mama Shari and Mama Lena were there too.

I was shaking and felt kind of scared.

Mama Lena picked me up and held me real close.

Mama Shari petted my head and kissed me.

Skipper kissed me too!

When I quit shaking I got in the big dog bed with Skipper. She let me snuggle real close even though sometimes she said I was too big for that.

"Do you remember what your dream was about Jack?" she asked.

At first, I didn't say anything. Thinking about that big scary dream was scary and made me shake again.

Skipper gave me kisses and put her leg around me.

"I was playing in our yard Skipper. Then the big tall fence fell down. I wanted to see Pax and Serenity. I looked in the yard and there was fire just like when I was puppy.

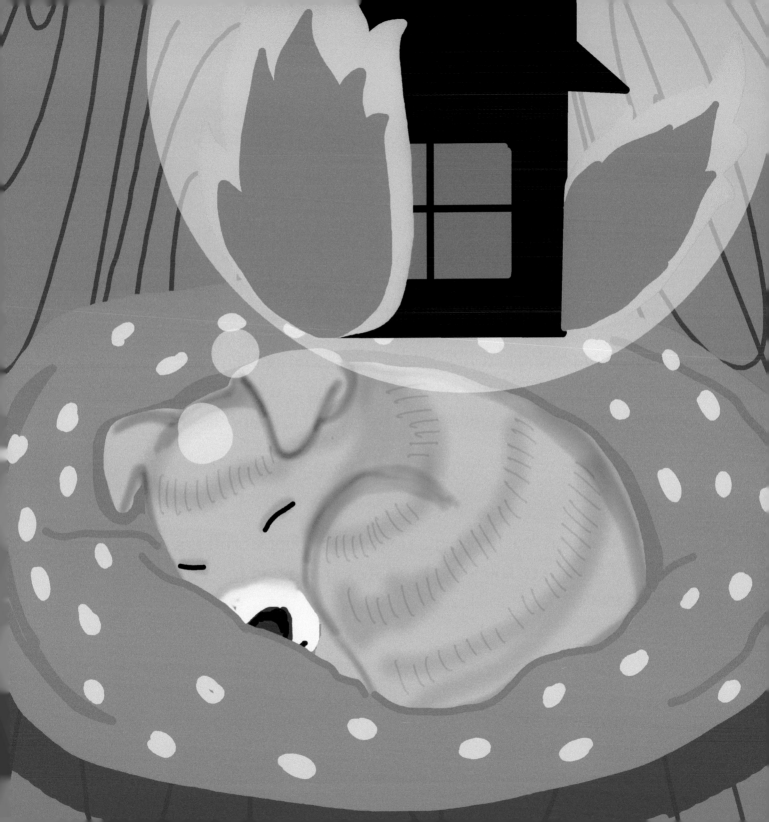

I heard my Mama Dog telling me to run. So, I ran. I ran as fast as my legs would go. I was looking for you. I was looking for Mama Shari and Mama Lena. Then I felt you kissing me and I opened my eyes Skipper. That was my big scary dream." I told her.

"I heard you crying and your legs were moving just like you were running but in your bed." Skipper said. "Mama Lena and Mama Shari heard you crying too. You're safe now Jack. No more big scary dreams."

She gave me another Skipper kiss. I snuggled real close to her in our big dog bed.

I thought about me, my Mama Dog and my puppy brothers and sisters. I hoped they were snuggling in a safe big dog bed too. I gave Skipper a kiss and went back to sleep.

The next morning when Skipper and I went outside I looked at the big tall fence.

I walked from one end of the big tall fence to the other.

I called Pax and Serenity but they did not answer.

I went and sat under the tree and looked at the big tall fence. I thought about my big scary dream.

Busta Cat was in his perch in the tree. He saw me looking at the big tall fence.

"What are you thinking about Jack?" he asked.

"I was thinking about this big tall fence Busta Cat. Why is it here? I don't think I like it Busta Cat. It made me have a big scary dream." I told him.

"Well you know it is in the way sort of. I mean I have to go two branches up, then jump over it and hope I land in just the right spot to visit Miss Midnight." He said.

"One time I landed in some cut grass and had to spend forever cleaning the fur suit off. A fellow can't go visiting all covered in grass. It's in the way Jack but not scary.

"Did you see fire when you visited Miss Midnight? Was there a fire pot?" I asked.

"No Jack. No fire. Just a big yard with dogs, humans and Miss Midnight at her window. That's all I see. You just had a bad dream Jack. The fence is in the way but its ok. There's Miss Midnight. Gotta go." Busta said and scooted up the tree so he could jump over the fence.

Skipper walked up just as Busta Cat got ready to jump over the fence. She barked "Busta's got a girlfriend! Busta's got a girlfriend!"

Busta Cat just hissed at her and jumped over the fence.

"I wish we could jump over the fence Skipper and play with Pax and Serenity" I said.

"Well maybe we can't jump over the fence but I'm working on a plan. Follow me." she said.

We went to the end of the fence where there was a big bush. Skipper took me behind the bush and showed me the plan.

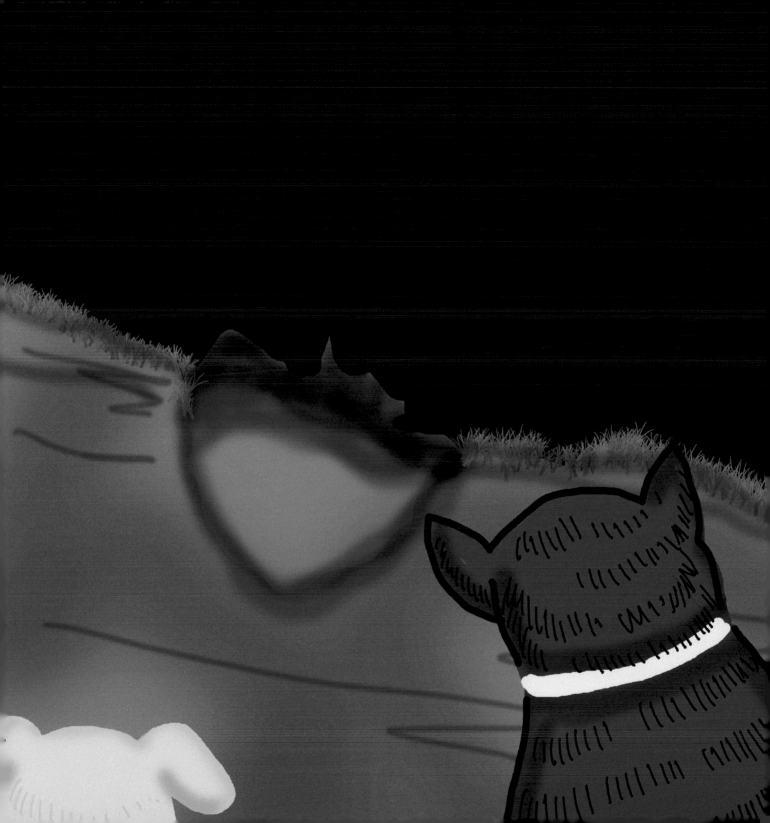

"If we dig right here pretty soon we will be able to go under the fence and play. See I have already started but it will go faster if we both dig." She said.

"But won't the mamas get mad." I asked. I remembered when I had dug a hole to bury one of my toys and Mama Lena had used the same voice that she had used when I chewed her shoe. I didn't like that voice.

"That's why we are digging here behind the bush. They'll never know." Skipper laughed. "Are you in or not?"

I thought about how much fun it would be to play with the dogs and maybe their boy too.

"I'm in Skipper!" I barked and we started to dig.

Skipper and I started our digging project behind the bush.

Serenity and Pax had come outside to play. They could hear us digging and came to the big tall fence.

"What are you doing?" they barked.

"We're digging under the fence so we can come play!" I said. I couldn't wait to play the sniffing game then run around the yard with Pax and Serenity.

"It was my idea!" Skipper said.

Pax and Serenity barked and Skipper and I dug faster.

I guess we were making lots of noise because Mama Shari came to the door and called us inside.

"Busted" Skipper said. She stopped digging and headed for the house.

I looked at Skipper and looked at our hole. We were almost there. I stuck my nose in the hole and then my head. If I dug just a little more I knew I could squeeze through the hole even without Skipper's help.

I heard Mama Shari calling but I heard Serenity and Pax too.

I really wanted to get to see them and to play so I started digging real fast.

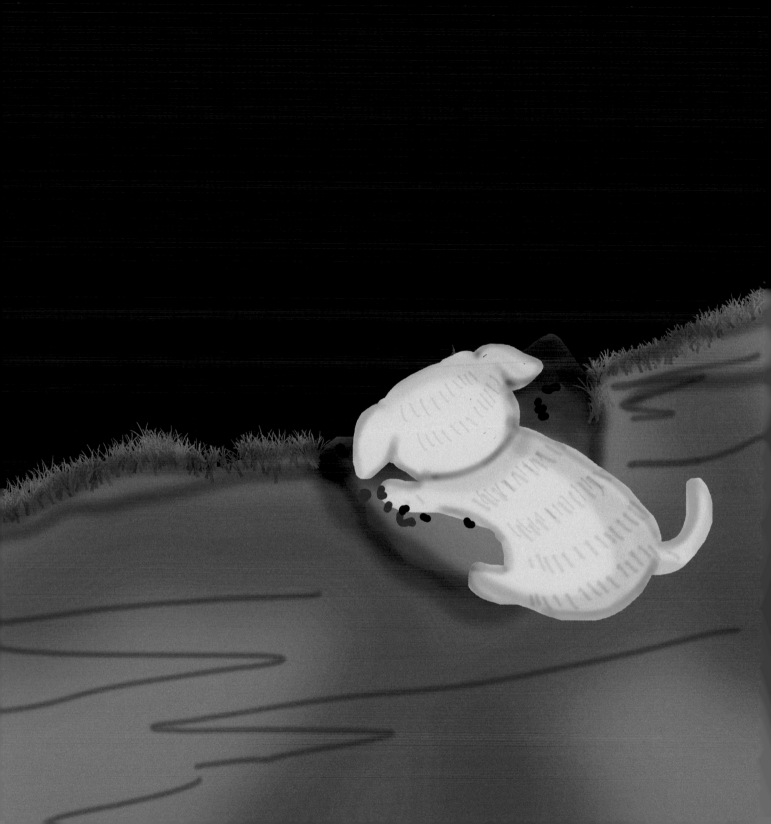

"Do you have to go in?" Pax asked.

"I'm almost there. I can do it" I answered.

"I'll help!' Pax said and I heard digging coming from the other side of the fence.

Mama Shari called again! But Pax and I just kept digging.

We were both digging real fast. The hole under the big tall fence was getting bigger and bigger.

First, I could get my nose under the fence then my head. Pretty soon I would be able to crawl under the big tall fence.

Mama Lena had come out on the porch and was calling me too.

Skipper ran to our secret digging spot and was barking at me. "You've got to stop Jack and come in now. If our mamas see the hole they'll be really upset. C'mon Jack!" she barked.

"I can't stop Skipper. I'm almost through." I said.

Pax barked "Don't stop Jack! I'll get my mom to help. You're almost through."

Skipper shook her head. "I'll hold them off as long as I can Jack but this is going to be trouble!" she barked and ran back towards the porch.

I could hear Pax barking but it wasn't to her human Mama, it was to Serenity.

"Hurry Mom! Jack's almost through and he needs our help" Pax was saying.

I heard both dogs running my way. I gave one big push on the ground with my back legs and I popped through the whole into their yard.

I barked, "I made it Pax! I'm here Serenity!' I brushed the dirt from my eyes and looked at the two dogs.

I saw the dogs running my way but I couldn't move. I couldn't believe my eyes.

The dogs began to speak but stopped.

"You made it Ja....." was all they could get out.

Slowly one of the dogs came over and gave me the sniff. I sniffed her back.

Then the smaller dog who had a curly tail just like me came over and sniffed me too.

"Puppy, is it really you?" the older dog asked. I knew it was Serenity from her voice.

"It is Puppy, Mama. Look he still has his curly tail just like me" the other dog said. I knew this dog was Pax by their voice.

"It's me! It's you!" I said.

I had found my dog family.

I could hear Mama Shari and Mama Lena calling me in their worried voices.

I wanted to go back through the hole under the big tall fence so they would know I was okay but I wanted to be with my dog family too.

The mamas were calling. Skipper was barking. They were on the other side of the fence by my hole but they were too big to come through.

"Maybe you better go back" my Mama dog said sadly.

"But our boy hasn't seen him yet Mama! Maybe if he sees puppy, I mean Jack, he will be happy too!" Pax said.

I remembered playing ball with the boy when I was just puppy! I wanted to play ball with him again.

I didn't want my human mammas to worry but I couldn't go back through the hole without seeing the boy.

"Jack come back." Skipper barked.

"I will Skipper but I have to see the boy." I barked.

I heard the mamas talking.

"C'mon Lena we've got to go get Jack. He's not coming back on his own."

"How embarrassing Shari. Here I was suggesting they would be bad neighbors for putting up the fence and its our pup who is trespassing on their property. So much for getting off to a good start. Let's go" Mama Lena said.

I heard the mamas and Skipper walk away from the hole in the fence.

Busta Cat was watching from his perch in the tree.

"Well things are about to get pretty interesting." He laughed. "I see why you and Pax look so much alike, Jack but how are you going to be with two families? Maybe they'll have to cut you in half."

"Cut me in half!! Oh no!' I cried.

"Don't pay him any attention Jack" my momma Serenity said. She looked at Busta Cat and growled "Not funny cat! Not funny!

She gave me a big kiss. "Stay here and play with Pax while I see if I can get the boy to come out." She said and headed toward the house.

Pax came over to play. "Let me show you around our yard. We missed you so much after the fire. How did you get to be Jack? How did you find your family?" she asked.

We took off running about the yard, smelling the flowers, marking some bushes and I told her my story.

Lena, Shari and Skipper rang the bell at the house next door.

"This is not how I wanted to meet our new neighbors. No welcome gift. No dish to share at a house warming, just us standing here on their doorstep to collect our wayward dog." Shari mumbled.

"I know right. And I had those incredibly stupid thoughts about them and that fence. I am so embarrassed." Lena replied.

Just then the door opened.

"Hello! We're Shari and Lena. We live next door." Shari said.

Skipper barked "What about me?"

"Sorry Skipper!" Shari said "And this is one of our dogs, Skipper."

"Well hello Skipper!" the woman said and bent down to scratch Skipper behind the ears.

"Hello ladies! I'm Susan It's nice to meet you" she said.

The man came to the door. "This is my husband Jim."

Lena said "Well this isn't totally a social call. Apparently, our other dog Jack couldn't wait for the formal introductions and has tunneled his way under the fence into your yard."

"We are so sorry. This is not the way we'd planned to welcome you to the neighborhood. Of course, we'll pay for any damages" Shari said with a nervous laugh.

"No worries! He's probably out there playing with our dogs. I'll have my son go get him" the woman said.

The boy was standing in the corner listening to everyone talk.

"Terrance these are our neighbors. Their dog is in the yard playing with Pax and Serenity would you mind getting him for them?' She asked.

The boy nodded yes and headed toward the back yard.

"Won't you come in and have a cool drink. It's been a long time since we had a proper home or neighbors really'"

"That would be great but don't go to any trouble. Some cold water would be enough" Shari said.

The women went into the living room and sat down. The man went in the kitchen and came back with four glasses of water and a small bowl of water on a tray.

He put the bowl of water down by Skipper. "Thought you might be thirsty too, little Miss." He said. Skipper gave him a kiss then laid down so he could scratch her belly.

"So cute!" the three women said all at the same time.

"There's enough Skipper to go around." Skipper barked and ran to each one so they could pet her.

The humans raised their glasses in a toast and said, "To new neighbors and new friends!"

Pax and I were playing in the yard. Pax was showing me their dog run on the other side of the yard.

We could hear Serenity barking at the door.

I heard the door open and the boy's voice say "Hate to break up the play date Serenity but your friend's moms have come to take him home. Where is he?"

"C'mon Jack! There he is. He's going to be so happy to see you. He really missed you. Almost as much as Mama and I did."

Pax and I took off running towards the porch. The boy was coming down the stairs.

He looked at Pax. He looked at me. He looked at Mama Dog.

"It can't be. Is it? Is it really you?" he said.

He sat on the ground and I ran over and gave him a big kiss. Pax gave him a big kiss.

Then Serenity came over. In her mouth was a yellow ball. She dropped it by the boy and gave him a kiss.

The boy picked up the ball and threw it.

"Do you remember boy? Do you remember me? Fetch the ball." He said.

I ran and got the ball and brought it back to him. He laughed. I barked. Serenity and Pax barked.

The boy laughed but water was coming from his eyes. He put this arms around me and gave me a big hug so I gave him a big kiss. Then Pax and Serenity started kissing him too.

We lay on the grass with the sun shining on us just smiling, laughing, barking and kissing.

I could hear Skipper barking at the door.

Skipper had finished drinking her water. She had been waiting in the living room for the boy to bring Jack in so they could go home.

She listened to the humans talk. The woman had gone and got the toddler. Her name wasn't toddler. It was Lillian but they called her Lilly! She put her on the floor. The toddler didn't pull Skipper's tail or make lots of noise.

Her mother said "Be gentle with Skipper, Lilly! Pet her softly. Skipper is your friend"

Skipper smiled. Now she had something else to tell Busta Cat. The toddler had a name, Lilly and Lilly was officially a friend of Skipper. Her mother had said so.

The boy had been gone for a while but instead of coming in with Jack there was lots of laughing and barking coming from the yard.

Skipper began barking and ran to the back door. The mother picked up Lilly and started towards the door.

"C'mon ladies! Looks like playing is going on out there, not dog wrangling." the father said.

He, Shari and Lena headed towards the back door.

The mother had let Skipper out into the yard but stood in the doorway holding Lilly. Water was coming from her eyes.

The father looked at Susan. The mamas looked at Susan. Then they looked out in the yard.

The boy, Serenity, Pax, Skipper and I were playing. The boy had a big smile on his face.

"Look Dad! Look!' he laughed pointing at me.

"Well, I'll be" the father said.

Mama Shari and Mama Lena looked confused.

"Remember when I told you ladies about the fire and how we got the dogs," the man explained." Well, what I left out was there was one little pup we lost. He and Pax were the only ones who looked just alike down to that curly tail. We thought he was gone for good. Broke Terrance's heart. But it looks like they've found each other again!"

I looked at Mama Shari and Mama Lena.

They were smiling but water was coming from their eyes now too.

The humans all hugged then sat on the porch to talk and watch us play.

After a while, Skipper's stomach went rumble, rumble. So did Pax's and Serenity's. Then my stomach rumbled.

Finally, the boy's stomach rumbled too.

"Hey mom, these guys are hungry! Me too." He said laughing.

"Oh my! It is that time. I haven't even started anything for dinner" she said.

Mama Shari said "Dinner's on us! After all it was our little trespasser that brought us all together."

"I can have homemade pizza ready in twenty minutes" Lena said. "Any special food requirements?" Lena said.

"Not a one. Pizza sounds great and let me make the salad." Jim Said.

"Terrance can bring the dogs. I'll bring my guitar. Lilly and I can provide the entertainment." Susan said laughing.

"Sounds like a plan" they all said together.

I stopped playing and ran over to everyone barking.

My mamas knelt down to pet me and I gave them both kisses.

"You can stay a little while longer Jack but then you have to come home for dinner" they said.

"What about me" Skipper barked. She and Serenity had started playing together. They both had on yellow bandanas.

Mama Lena reached down to pet Skipper and Serenity. She noticed Serenity had on a bandana just like Skippers.

"OK Skipper you can stay too!" Mama Lena said.

When the boy said it was time for dinner, I headed for my tunnel to go back under the fence.

Skipper, Serenity and Pax just stood and looked at me.

"C'mon! Aren't you hungry? Follow me" I barked.

"I don't think that hole is big enough for all of us Jack" Serenity said.

"We could make it bigger" I barked.

Pax looked at me and at the hole. "I guess we could make it bigger Jack but that might take a long time. And I don't think everyone wants to get dirty." Pax said and looked at Skipper and Serenity in their bandanas.

"That's right! Some of us have on accessories. We can't be digging through that dirt." Skipper said.

Just then the boy walked up.

"What's going on dogs? Foods this way. Let's go!' He said and started walking back towards the house.

Skipper and Serenity ran along beside the boy, but Pax and I stood by the hole and barked.

The boy stopped walking and looked at us.

The man came out and asked what all the noise was about.

"I think Jack and Pax want to take their short cut next-door Dad." The boy said.

The man looked at us. He looked at the hole then he looked at the big, tall fence.

He pushed on the fence where we had made our hole and it moved a little bit.

"Hmm. That's not good. Probably not a safe spot for two little dogs to be scooting back forth." He said.

"Should I get the shovel and fill in the hole Dad?" the boy asked.

"No son. They'd just dig under it again. Bring me my hammer and the crowbar. I have an idea.

The boy ran to the garage and came back with the tools.

"You use the hammer son and pound in any loose nails when I pry these boards loose." He said.

We could hear the mamas talking on the other side of the fence. Lilly was there too. Her mama was making music.

We could smell the food too!

Our stomachs rumbled louder.

The boy and the man were hitting and pounding on the big, tall fence. Then all of a sudden, right above the place where Pax and I had dug the hole, the big, tall fence fell down into the yard.

Pax, Serenity, Skipper and I ran through from their yard to our yard. Then the boy stepped through.

The three mamas looked at us then at the fence

"Well ladies what do you think? A doggie door seems appropriate after all we are all kind of sort of family." the man said laughing as he came through the space in the fence.

Mama Shari put the birthday tablecloth on the table even though it wasn't country's birthday anymore.

Mama Lena brought out the pizza and put it on the table by the salad.

The boy had brought Pax and Serenity's bowl to our house. He put food in their bowls and ours.

Busta Cat had been in his perch watching.

"Good job dogs! I knew you'd do something about that fence. Now can you get Miss Midnight out of the house so we can have some fun too! I'm just saying love is love so send some a cat's way" he said.

He climbed down and walked through the space in the fence to visit Miss Midnight.

After we had finished eating Terrance's mom sang songs and the toddler Lilly tried to sing too. Skipper, Pax and I threw our heads back and joined in.

The man Jim sat with Mama Shari and Mama Lena just watching.

Serenity came and sat at his feet.

"Seems like it was a lifetime ago, I told this girl that one day all of us, me and mine and her with all of her pups were going to have a real home." He said petting Serenity.

"I made sure all the pups found a good home. Couldn't give Serenity and Pax away. They're part of the family. When Lilly came, I would watch how gentle both dogs were with the baby. Serenity was so protective. But the loss of that one little pup, well it left a whole in our hearts." He said. "but look at him! Her pup is alive and well."

"Jack is our sweet boy," Mama Shari said. "You don't want him back. Do you?"

"You could leave the space in the fence so he could go back and forth. We wouldn't mind. This is his home." Mama Lena said.

"I can see that. He's happy, healthy and loved. This is his home but about the fence?"

"Yes? Both mommas said together.

"Well," Jim said "let's skip the doggie door and make it a family path since we are all kind of, sort of Jack's extended family. What do you think?"

Mama Lena got up and went to the table. She started pouring lemonade into five glasses and a little bit into Lilly's sippy cup.

"Terrance, will you put some water in the bowls for the dogs" she asked and our boy grabbed the hose and quickly filled up our four bowls.

I knew what came next.

She passed out the drinks then raised her glass.

"Let's have a toast to Jack with the Curly tail who has brought so much love and joy to all of us!" she said.

"And to getting to know and grow with Jim, Susan, Terrance and Lilly as neighbors and family!" Shari said.

"Let's not forget the dogs" Jim said.

Susan gave Lilly her sippy cup then raised her glass "To families, big and small.

The humans drank their lemonade.

We dogs drank our water.

Skipper came over and asked me what I was thinking about.

"Well Skipper I was thinking about a lot of things. I lost one family. I found a new family. I made new friends. I went from being puppy to Jack. It's like all my big dreams but happy." I said.

"This isn't a dream is it Skipper"

Skipper reached over and nipped my paw.

"Ouch! Why'd you do that Skipper?" I asked.

"Just so you'd know it's not a dream Jack. You're here and we are one big family" She said.

I looked around the yard. There was Mama Shari, Mama Lena, Jim, Susan, Lilly, Serenity, Pax and Skipper.

Just then my boy Terrance rolled the ball to me just like when I was puppy.

"Want to play Jack?" he said smiling at me.

And just like when I was "Puppy" I grabbed that ball and we began to play.